World Famous
MURIEL

World Famous
MURIEL

by Sue Alexander

Pictures by Chris L. Demarest

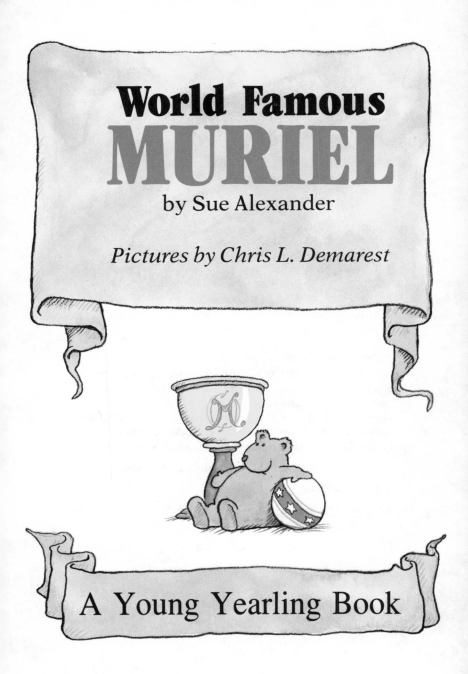

A Young Yearling Book

Published by
Dell Publishing Co., Inc.
1 Dag Hammarskjold Plaza
New York, New York 10017

Yearling ® TM 913705, Dell Publishing Co., Inc.

ISBN: 0-440-40024-4

Reprinted by arrangement with Little, Brown and Com-
pany, Inc.

Printed in the United States of America

January 1988

10 9 8 7 6 5 4 3 2 1

W

For Jane Yolen:
Nurturer, encourager, and dear friend

S.A.

For Anna

C.L.D.

Muriel is the best tightrope walker
in the world.
She is World Famous.

When Kings, Queens, or Presidents
want to see someone
walk a tightrope,
they call Muriel.

Muriel is also very smart.
She is World Famous for that, too.
When doctors, teachers,
or judges need someone
to solve very hard problems,
they call Muriel.

One day a Queen called Muriel.
"Muriel," said the Queen,
"tomorrow is my birthday.
I am having a party.
I have invited
some very important people.
Now I am inviting you.
Will you come to my party
and walk on your tightrope?"

Muriel thought.
"Are you going to serve
peanut butter cookies?" she asked.

"Of course," said the Queen.
"Then I will come," Muriel said.

The next afternoon,
Muriel put on her new costume.

And off she went.

"No," sobbed the Queen.
"It's my paper lanterns.
I hung them on the trees
to make the yard look pretty.

The Queen stopped crying.
She looked at Muriel.
"Muriel," she said,
"you are the best tightrope walker
in the world.
You are World Famous.
You are also very smart.
You are World Famous for that, too.
Will you find my paper lanterns?"

"I'll be glad to," said Muriel.
"I will think very hard.
I will think of who took them.
Then I will know where to find them."
"Good!" said the Queen.

Muriel ate a cookie.
Then she walked around the yard.
The Queen followed her.

Muriel stopped.
"I have thought of
who could have taken your lanterns,"
she said.

"Who?" asked the Queen.

"Someone with big feet," said Muriel.
"We are standing in a footprint."
The Queen looked down.
"Oh my," she said. "So we are."

"That is good thinking.
You *are* smart, Muriel,"
said the Queen.
"I know," said Muriel.
And she ate another cookie.

Then she looked
for another footprint.
She found three of them.
"I have thought of something,"
Muriel said.
"This someone has *four* big feet."

"Oh my," said the Queen.

Muriel followed the footprints.
The Queen followed Muriel.
They went out of the gate
and away from the castle.

Then Muriel saw something else.
She saw two pink feathers.
"I have thought of something,"
Muriel said.
"This someone has four big feet
and pink feathers."
"Oh, dear!" said the Queen.

Muriel followed more footprints
and pink feathers.
Suddenly she slid to a stop.
"What is it, Muriel?"
asked the Queen.

"I have thought of something,"
Muriel said.

"This someone has four big feet,
pink feathers,
and likes bananas."
"How do you know?" asked the Queen.
"I just slipped on a banana peel,"
said Muriel.
"Oh," said the Queen.

Muriel followed the footprints,
pink feathers,
and banana peels.
The Queen followed Muriel.

Muriel ate more cookies.
Then she said,
"I know where to find your lanterns."
And off she went.
The Queen went after her.

Muriel went up one road

and down another.

Then she stopped.

"Muriel, this is the zoo!"
said the Queen.

"Yes," Muriel said.
"And your lanterns are inside."
The Queen went to look.

Her paper lanterns were hanging
from the elephant's fence
and near the flamingo's pond
and on the monkey's cage.

"Oh my," said the Queen.
"How did you know they were here?"
"I thought very hard," Muriel said.

"I thought that no *one* someone has
four big feet,
pink feathers,
and likes bananas."
"That's a relief!" said the Queen.

"And if it was not *one* someone,"
Muriel went on,
"it had to be *three* someones.
Elephants have four big feet.
Flamingos have pink feathers.
And monkeys like bananas.
They all live at the zoo.
That's how I knew
your lanterns were here."

"Oh, Muriel, you are so smart!"
said the Queen.
"I know," said Muriel.
And she ate another cookie.

"But I don't understand,"
said the Queen.
"*Why* did they take them?"
"Because," Muriel said,
"your lanterns are pretty.
And everyone needs to have
pretty things to look at."

"Oh," said the Queen.
She looked around.
"Now the zoo is prettier
than my backyard," she said.
And she sighed.

"Well then," Muriel said,
"there's only one thing to do."
"What?" asked the Queen.

"Have your party here at the zoo,"
answered Muriel.
And she ate another cookie.
"That's a wonderful idea!"
said the Queen.

The animals thought so, too.

Muriel is the best tightrope walker
in the world.
She is World Famous.
Muriel is also very smart.
She is World Famous for that.
Muriel can eat a lot of cookies.

Maybe someday she will be
World Famous
for that, too.